The Boxcar Children® Mysteries

THE GYMNASTICS MYSTERY

created by
GERTRUDE CHANDLER WARNER

Illustrated by Charles Tang

ALBERT WHITMAN & Company
Morton Grove, Illinois

Library of Congress Cataloging-in-Publication Data

Warner, Gertrude Chandler, 1890-1979
The gymnastics mystery/
created by Gertrude Chandler Warner;
illustrated by Charles Tang.
p. cm. — (The Boxcar Children mysteries)
Summary: The Aldens try to help a visiting Russian gymnast who is
surrounded by mysterious people and events and who seems to have a secret.
ISBN 0-8075-3100-6(hardcover)—
ISBN 0-8075-3101-4(paperback)
[1. Gymnastics—Fiction. 2.. Brothers and sisters—Fiction.
3. Orphans—Fiction. 4. Mystery and detective stories.]
I. Tang, Charles, ill. II. Title.
III. Series: Warner, Gertrude Chandler, 1890-
Boxcar children mysteries.
PZ7.W244Gy 2000   99-043098
[Fic]—dc21   CIP

Cover art by David Cunningham.

THE GYMNASTICS
MYSTERY

Contents

CHAPTER 1

The Girl from Russia

Six-year-old Benny Alden held up a sign with KATYA LUDSKAYA written on it. He watched anxiously as passengers walked through the airport doorway.

"What if we miss her?" he said to his sister Jessie.

"We won't," Jessie replied. At twelve, she was the most organized of the Alden children. She had made the sign. "We know Katya is on this plane."

"But we don't know what she looks like,"

Benny said. "And she doesn't know what *we* look like."

"That's why Jessie made the sign," said Henry, the oldest at fourteen. "Her coach told us Katya reads and speaks English. She'll see the card and come over to us."

Violet Alden leaned over Benny's shoulder. The Russian girl they were waiting for was ten years old, exactly her age. She was as excited as her little brother to see their houseguest.

"The crowd is thinning out," Jessie observed. "Katya was probably sitting in the back of the plane."

"This was a long journey," Grandfather said. "Katya flew from Russia to New York, then changed planes for this flight to Hartford. And we still have to drive home."

In just a few days, their hometown of Greenfield, Connecticut, was hosting a gymnastics competition in the new Greenfield Sports Arena. James Alden had offered to sponsor one of the foreign gymnasts. Many athletes relied on people like Grandfather to let them stay in their homes. Otherwise, they couldn't afford to compete in other countries.

"That must be her!" Benny cried, spying a small blond girl. She wore a blue warm-up suit and carried a red sports bag.

The girl scanned the waiting area with worried blue eyes. Then she saw Benny holding the sign with her name on it and smiled with relief.

The Aldens hurried forward.

"Hi!" Benny said. "Are you Katya?"

"Yes, I am Katya Ludskaya," the girl replied. "And you are Benny, yes?" She pronounced Benny's name *Bennee*.

Grandfather held out his hand. "I'm James Alden, Katya. Welcome to the United States."

"Thank you so much," Katya said shyly. "This is my first time in your country."

"Well, let's get your luggage and drive home," said Grandfather. "Then you can see more of America than the inside of an airport."

Violet was surprised that Katya was only a little taller than Benny. She was enchanted by the Russian girl's accent and her beautiful smile.

"I'm Violet Alden," she said. "Can I carry your bag?"

Katya gave her the red sports bag. "Thank you, Violet."

"I'm Jessie," Jessie said as they rode the escalator down to the baggage claim area. "And this is Henry."

"We're glad you're staying with us," added Henry.

"I am so happy you are having me stay," Katya said.

Benny half turned on the moving stairs to look back. "Mrs. McGregor is cooking a special dinner tonight for you. Hamburgers and french fries and pie!"

Katya seemed pleased and a little less shy. "Real American food! How wonderful."

Downstairs, they walked over to the carousel, where suitcases, boxes, and bags from Katya's flight were going around on a conveyor belt.

"I hope I have not missed mine," Katya said, concerned.

"Don't worry," said Henry. "It'll take a while to unload all the luggage from the plane. What does your suitcase look like?"

"It is black," Katya replied. "With squashy sides. I don't know what you call it — "

"Is it like that one?" Jessie pointed to a green duffel bag.

"Yes, only black." Then Katya cried, "There it is!"

But as she reached for the black duffel, a man with black hair and a yellow cap pushed past her and grabbed it.

"Hey!" Benny cried, but the man had already left.

Grandfather pointed to the carousel. "That bag belonged to that man. There are lots of black duffels, Katya. We'll have to check them all."

"*This* one is mine," said Katya when another black duffel came around. "I am sure of it."

Relieved that they'd finally found the right bag, Henry grabbed it quickly before it passed. "Got it."

"Now we can go home," Benny told Katya. "I hope you like our house. We have a dog named Watch, but he's real friendly — "

"Benny," Jessie said, laughing. "Katya will be with us all week."

"That's okay, Benny," said Katya. "I want to hear about Watch and anything else you would like to tell me."

Henry shifted Katya's bag to his other hand. "We want to hear about your family, too."

"What is your house like?" asked Violet.

Instead of answering, Katya said, "What kind of pie are we having for dinner?"

"Apple," Jessie replied as they passed pay phones and lockers built into the wall.

She noticed the man in the yellow cap. He was hanging up the handset of a pay phone, the duffel on the floor by his feet.

Nearby a scruffy-looking younger man with light hair slouched with a dog at his side. He looked as if he were waiting for the phone the older man had just finished using. The young man crouched down to pet his dog. "You hungry, Ralphie?" he said softly. "Don't worry, boy, I'll get you some dinner. Promise."

Weird, thought Jessie. There were at least a dozen unoccupied telephones. The scruffy young man was obviously making the older man nervous by standing too close. As the older man hung up the handset and stepped away from the phone, he backed into the Alden children and Katya.

"Sorry," he apologized. Then, as his glance took in Katya, his eyes widened as if he had seen a ghost. As he quickly snatched up his bag and hurried out the door to the taxi line, a small key fell from his hand to the floor.

Grandfather was leading Katya out the same door.

Henry dropped back to speak to the others. "Did that guy seem weird or what?"

"Definitely weird," confirmed Violet. "I wonder why he was staring at us that way."

Jessie shook her head. "I don't know. I've never seen him before."

While his brother and sisters were discussing the stranger's odd behavior, Benny picked up the tiny silver key he had seen the stranger drop. It had a small number 17 stamped on it.

Before Benny could mention his find, the young man with the dog rushed by them and out the door.

"Everybody's certainly in a hurry," said Violet. "I guess he's afraid his mysterious friend will leave him."

"Who knows?" Henry shrugged. "We'd better hurry ourselves. Grandfather and Katya will be at the car by now. Come on, Benny."

Benny slipped the key in his pocket and promptly forgot about it. He planned to sit beside Katya in Grandfather's big station wagon and show her the sights.

Within minutes, the Aldens and their houseguest had left the airport behind and were heading toward Greenfield.

"The United States is so big," commented Katya, looking at everything with interest. "And so pretty."

"Russia is much bigger," Grandfather said. "What part do you come from?"

"Oh, a little town near St. Petersburg," Katya replied vaguely. "The towns here are like pictures in a book. I can spell Connecticut!" And she did, proudly.

Benny was impressed. "Boy, I can't even spell Connecticut, and I live here!"

Everyone laughed. Then Jessie and Henry taught Katya "Michael, Row the Boat Ashore," and they sang the rest of the way to Greenfield.

As Grandfather pulled the station wagon into the driveway, the large white house came into view.

"Is this your house?" said Katya. "For just the five of you?"

"And Mrs. McGregor," said Jessie, swinging open the car door.

"And Watch," Benny added.

At that moment, the dog bounded out the front door, barking in greeting. Katya giggled when Watch eagerly licked her hand.

"He likes me!" she said, delighted.

Mrs. McGregor came out to welcome their guest.

"I hope your visit will be comfortable," the housekeeper said, opening the door wide.

Katya smiled shyly again. "I am sure it will be."

Upstairs, she stopped when she saw the guest room.

"Is this for me?" she asked in amazement.

The room, which overlooked the back-yard, was furnished with a canopied four-poster bed. A quilt sewn in pink and green blocks made the bed even more inviting. Mrs. McGregor had arranged dried cattails in a green pottery vase.

"The bed belonged to Grandfather's mother," said Henry, putting Katya's bag on the floor by the dresser. "It's old."

"But it won't fall down or anything," Benny put in, making them all laugh again.

Katya went over to the large window and drew back the lace curtain. "What is that?" she inquired. "It looks like a train car!"

"It is," said Violet. "We'll tell you about

it at dinner. I'm sure you want to wash up and rest a little."

Then the children left and went downstairs to help Mrs. McGregor with dinner.

In addition to hamburgers and french fries, the housekeeper fixed baked beans, hot dogs, and coleslaw. Two fragrant apple pies cooled on the countertop.

When it was time to eat, everyone filed into the dining room.

"Sit by me," Benny begged Katya.

"All right," said Katya, unfolding her napkin in her lap. "Everything smells so good!"

"Dig in," said Grandfather, passing the plate of meat to the guest. "Mrs. McGregor outdid herself."

"Oh, it's nothing," said Mrs. McGregor. "Just hamburgers and hot dogs."

Katya speared a hot dog from the plate. "Where I come from, we never have two kinds of meat at the same time. Americans are so lucky! You are all rich!"

"Not all Americans are rich," Grandfather said gently.

"And we didn't always have a lot of food,"

Henry broke in. "And we didn't always live in this house. In fact, we didn't have a home at all for a while."

Katya stared at him. "That is not so!"

"Yes, it is," said Jessie. "You see, our parents died suddenly and we didn't have anyplace to go. We didn't know about Grandfather then."

Violet took up the story. "So we found this boxcar in the woods and lived in that. Henry earned money for food."

"Then Grandfather found us," said Benny. "He had been looking for us, and we thought he was mean. But he isn't and he took us to live here."

Katya looked confused. "I do not understand."

"My grandchildren heard things about me that weren't true," explained James Alden. "They hid in that boxcar. But then I found them and brought them here to live with me. We've been happy ever since."

"And we've solved a lot of mysteries," said Benny.

Grandfather laughed. "Benny is right. These four are quite good detectives."

"What an amazing family!" Katya declared.

When dinner was over, the Aldens took her outside to show her the boxcar.

It was getting dark when they went back in the house.

"Katya, you must be exhausted," said Mrs. McGregor. "Jessie and Violet will help you get settled in."

Jessie led the way upstairs to the guest room.

Katya picked up her duffel bag and placed it on the bed. She unzipped the top, then gasped.

"What is it?" Violet asked, concerned.

Katya pulled out a man's tie. "This bag! It is not mine!"

CHAPTER 2

The Wrong Bag

"Are you sure?" Violet asked.

"Yes! These are all men's clothes!" Katya pulled out another tie and a pair of shoes, then stuffed the items back into the duffel. "What am I going to do?"

At that moment, Henry and Benny stopped by the door.

"Everything okay?" Henry asked.

"No, it isn't," answered Jessie. "Katya picked up the wrong bag at the airport. This one has men's things in it."

"That was an easy mistake to make,"

Benny said to Katya. He put a comforting hand on her shoulder. "There were lots of black bags just like yours on that merry-go-round."

"I know," she said, on the verge of tears. "But I should have checked the tag. I was so excited — "

Jessie grabbed the luggage tag hanging from the strap. "This bag belongs to Al Stockton. He lives in Rockwell."

"That's the next town over," Violet said.

Now Grandfather came by. "I see long faces in here. What's the matter?"

Jessie explained about the bag mix-up.

Grandfather looked at the tag and said, "Mr. Stockton only has his address on here. No phone number. So we'll deliver his bag to Rockwell tomorrow after breakfast."

"Do you think he has mine?" Katya asked anxiously.

"It's possible," Grandfather assured her. "Your coach told me your luggage would have our address on the tag. Whoever has it will surely return it. Now let's all get some rest and tackle this problem in the morning."

"We'll lend you things for the night," Jessie offered. "There are extra toothbrushes in the bathroom. And a pair of Violet's pajamas will be a little large but will do for now."

"Thank you," said Katya, blinking back tears. "I'm sorry to be so much trouble."

"Don't worry about it," said Grandfather. "We want you to concentrate on the competition and do your best."

The next morning was sunny but cold. Mrs. McGregor cooked a hearty breakfast of French toast, poached eggs, and sausage patties.

"This ought to chase the chill away," the housekeeper said, setting platters on the table.

Benny sat next to Katya again. "Mrs. McGregor makes the best French toast." He handed the plate to her first, even though he was very hungry.

Before anyone could take a single bite, the doorbell rang insistently. Mrs. McGregor left to answer it. She came back leading a tall, black-haired man. He wore a yellow cap and carried a dusty duffel.

Violet realized instantly it was the mysterious man from the airport the day before.

"You!" the man accused Katya. "You took my bag!"

Katya shrank in her chair, frightened by his blustering manner.

"Now, see here." Grandfather pushed away from the table. "Speak in a civil tone when you are in my home. And please announce yourself."

"Al Stockton. I'm returning this." He thrust the bag at Katya.

"My bag!" she cried. "Thank you so much."

"Where's mine? Do you have it?" Al demanded.

Katya sprang to her feet. "Yes, I do. I'll get it right away." She ran upstairs with her own bag.

"We were on our way to your house as

soon as we had finished breakfast," Grandfather told Mr. Stockton. "Since your phone
number wasn't on your luggage tag, we
weren't able to call."

"You're lucky," Henry added. "You picked
up Katya's bag and she picked up yours
by mistake. Someone else could have had
yours."

Katya returned with Mr. Stockton's duffel. He practically snatched it out of her
hands.

"Did you go through my stuff?" he inquired.

Jessie came to their guest's defense. "We
only unzipped the bag and saw enough to
know it wasn't Katya's."

"I think an apology is in order," Grandfather prodded.

"Sorry," Mr. Stockton mumbled gruffly.

Benny noticed the mystery man couldn't
look at Katya. It was almost as if he were
afraid of her. But why?

Then Benny remembered the tiny silver
key he had found at the airport. He was
sure Mr. Stockton had dropped it. But be-

fore Benny could mention it, the man was gone.

"What a strange man," Henry observed. He added to Katya, "Not all Americans are like Mr. Stockton."

She smiled. "Not all Russians are so nice, either."

It was time to drive Katya to the arena. She changed into a blue-and-white warm-up suit and carried a water bottle and her sports bag. The Aldens were excited at the idea of watching a professional gymnast practice.

Grandfather let them off at the main entrance to the sports facility, promising to return when Katya's morning session was over.

When they entered the huge arena, the Alden children stared in astonishment. Everywhere young people flipped over bars, performed handstands on thin poles, and cartwheeled across thick blue mats.

"Wow!" exclaimed Benny. "It's like those people at the circus. What do you call them?"

"Acrobats," Henry replied.

"Some of the tricks we do in gymnastics are what acrobats do," said Katya. "There's my coach!"

A woman with short blond hair strode over with a clipboard. "Katya," she said in the same accent as Katya's. "I'm so glad to see you. Are you ready to begin?"

"Yes. These are the Aldens, the family I am staying with." She introduced Henry, Jessie, Violet, and Benny to her coach, who was named Irina.

"Is it okay if we watch?" Jessie asked. The athletes were practicing for a serious competition, she knew. Maybe they didn't like outsiders around while they worked.

"Of course," said Irina. "Gymnasts are used to spectators. Katya will warm up and stretch first. Then she will go through her sets on the balance beam and the uneven parallel bars."

Taking off her blue-and-white jacket, Katya laid it on a bleacher seat. Then she stepped out of the pants and took off her shoes and socks.

Dressed in a matching blue-and-white leotard, the girl seemed tinier than ever, Violet thought. But her legs and shoulders looked strong.

Katya joined the other members of her team. The Aldens found seats in the bleachers near where the team was working.

"I have to condition first," Katya told them from the mat. "If I don't, I could pull a muscle and hurt myself."

She did sit-ups, push-ups, and ran around the arena. When she returned from her run, she sat on the mat and stretched.

"These exercises keep my muscles limber," she said, sitting so her legs were straight out to her sides. "This is called a straddle split."

After warming up, Katya went over to the balance beam. The Aldens were in awe as Katya leaped lightly onto the narrow beam and performed tricks on it. Her coach stood nearby, in case she fell.

Next Katya did her routine on the uneven parallel bars. These were two bars set at different heights. Katya rubbed chalk on her hands so she wouldn't slip, then swung from the lowest bar. Her legs split as she flipped completely over, catching her hands on the higher bar.

"Look at that!" gasped Benny.

"She's great," Henry agreed.

When the session was over, a breathless Katya joined the Aldens. She immediately pulled on her warm-up suit.

"So my muscles will not get cold," she explained.

"Can you teach me to do that?" Benny asked.

Katya laughed. "Well, maybe one or two things."

"Yippee!" Benny was delighted.

They left the arena and walked out to the curb, where Grandfather was waiting in the station wagon.

"How did it go?" he asked.

"Katya is the best one," Benny stated. "She's going to teach me to be a gymnast, too. How long will it take?"

"About five years," Katya replied.

"Oh," said Benny thoughtfully. "Can you stay with us that long?"

Grandfather, the older Alden children, and Katya burst into laughter. Benny looked disappointed.

Back home, they all sat down to a lunch of tomato soup and grilled cheese sandwiches. Katya explained how she had been training since she was younger than Benny.

"I won my first competition when I was six," she said.

"That's how old I am now," Benny said, dismayed.

"But Katya had been training for years," Grandfather reminded him.

Jessie tried to imagine being so good at something at such a young age. "How do you train?"

"I go to the gym every day," Katya replied. "I work with Irina at least five hours. Then I go to school. After school, I work another hour or two at home. My father built a low balance beam, only a few inches off the floor. So I can work without worrying about falling."

"Whew!" Henry commented. "That's a lot of hard work."

"Yes, but I enjoy it," said Katya. "My home — " She broke off suddenly.

"What about your home?" Violet urged.

Katya stared into her soup bowl. "It is nothing. I am chattering too much."

Grandfather reviewed a sheet Katya's coach had sent him. "Katya is supposed to rest after lunch. Then we'll take her back to the arena for her afternoon workout."

"Do you have to do this every day?" asked Violet.

Katya nodded. "It is the way our team prepares for competitions. But I have free time after my second practice."

"We'll do something fun," Jessie promised. "You can't work every second!"

When Katya went upstairs to take a nap, the Alden children cleared the table.

"I wonder why Katya quit talking about her parents," mused Violet. "She hasn't told us anything about her home in Russia yet."

Henry stacked soup bowls. "She hasn't had much time, Violet. Maybe she'll tell us tonight when we go out."

But Violet remembered yesterday when she asked Katya the same question. *Why did Katya avoid talking about herself and her life back in Russia?* she wondered.

The afternoon session at the arena was just as hectic. Boys and girls twisted, flipped, and spun around on bars, rings, beams, and mats.

Once again, Katya removed her warm-up suit as the Aldens found seats nearby on the bleachers.

An American girl about Katya's age was stretching on the mat. She was close enough to the bleachers that the Aldens could hear her speak to Katya.

"Hi," said the girl.

"Hello," Katya replied.

"My name is Denise," said the American. "I think our teams are competing against each other."

"We are in the same class?" asked Katya. "Well, I wish you the best of luck."

At that moment, Denise's mother swooped down from the bleachers. She took Denise by the hand and led her across the room.

The Aldens came to the edge of the mat where Katya was now stretching alone.

"What happened?" asked Benny. "Why did she make Denise leave?"

"Some people think we should be enemies just because we are competing on different teams," Katya replied matter-of-factly.

Irina came over then and helped Katya perform different vaults over a leather-padded, barrel-shaped piece of equipment about chest high. Irina called it a horse. The Aldens held their breath as Katya ran as hard as she could toward the horse, then sprang off a short board. After pushing off the horse, she tucked her body tightly into a ball, spun once high in midair, and then untucked and came down lightly on her feet, her body straight as a pole.

When she landed, arms up, she took a small step back to catch her balance.

"Stick the landing. You know, stand firm and still when you land," Irina chided. "The judges will subtract points if you step off."

Katya nodded. "I will do better."

Her last workout was the floor routine. While music played from a tape deck, Katya turned, cartwheeled, and somersaulted across the wide blue mat.

"That's what I want to do!" Benny declared.

Katya came over, mopping her face with a towel. "Did you enjoy that? My coach and I worked very hard to put together a routine to that piece of music."

"It looks so hard," Violet said.

Their guest grinned. "It is actually the most fun." She reached for the pants of her warm-up suit, then frowned. "Where is my jacket?"

Violet spotted the blue garment crumpled on the floor. When she picked it up, she saw the jacket was wet.

"Oh, no," groaned Katya. "There is

water all over my jacket. How will I keep warm now?"

"You can borrow mine," Henry offered. His coat was too big, but at least Katya wouldn't catch cold.

Jessie found Katya's water bottle under the bleachers.

"Look," she said. "The bottle is empty, but the cap is on! Someone must have poured water on Katya's jacket, then put the cap back on."

"Why would anyone do that?" asked Violet.

As the Aldens left, Jessie scanned the bleachers around the arena. She didn't see Denise's blond mother, only a red-haired woman wearing blue sweatpants and matching sweatshirt. The woman was watching them.

Could she have poured water all over Katya's warm-up suit? Jessie wondered.

If so, *why?*

CHAPTER 3

Katya's Secret

"Mmm! This is very good," said Katya as she nibbled on a slice of pizza.

"Joe's has the best pizza in the town square," Jessie agreed, sampling a piece of pepperoni.

"I like everybody's pizza," Benny put in. He had cheese stuck to his chin.

Violet laughed, handing him a paper napkin. "That's true. Benny hasn't met a piece of pizza he didn't like."

"What do you think of our town?" Henry asked Katya.

"It is very pretty," Katya replied.

The children had decided that Katya would enjoy walking around the town square after her long day of practice. Mrs. McGregor had fixed a light supper so they wouldn't be too full for treats like pizza and ice cream. Then Grandfather drove them into town, giving Jessie spending money.

Although it was dark outside, the square was brightly lit and all the shops were open.

The children walked around, gazing into shop windows. Then Benny said he smelled pizza and didn't it smell great. They all agreed and followed their noses to Joe's Pizza. The delicious pizza smell had made them all hungry again.

"I could *sleep* in here, it's so nice and warm," Benny said after finishing two slices.

Katya laughed. "I agree, though I do not mind the cold so much. Our Russian winters are far worse."

"Tell us about your hometown," Henry asked.

"There is not much to say," Katya replied vaguely. "I come from a small place. I have parents, a brother, a sister, and grandparents."

"What are they like?" Jessie wanted to know.

"They are not very interesting," Katya said, shredding her napkin. Jessie wondered why the girl was so nervous all of a sudden. "Could I have a glass of water?" Katya asked.

"Of course." Henry got up to fetch Katya some water.

Jessie went with him, carrying paper plates. Away from the table, she whispered, "What's wrong with Katya?"

"I don't know," Henry said in a low voice. "Whenever we ask her anything about Russia, she changes the subject."

"It's pretty mysterious," Jessie said.

"We'd better get back," Henry said. "The others will wonder what we're talking about."

Outside again, the children strolled around the square. Katya was fascinated by a shop that sold only teddy bears.

"Look at that bear with the big red bow," she remarked, pointing at a large bear in the window. "He is so cute!"

"I have a stuffed bear," Benny told her. "Watch is jealous of him."

That made everyone laugh.

As they walked along, Henry had an odd feeling. The streetlamps cast long shadows in front of them. Henry noticed a sixth shadow apart from their group.

Whenever they stopped to look at something, light footsteps behind them stopped, too.

Using the reflection of a jewelry store window, Henry saw a figure in a baseball cap hiding behind a tree. They moved on again, the figure trailing them.

They were being followed! Suddenly Henry whirled around. Just as quickly, the figure ducked inside a yogurt shop.

"What are you doing?" Violet asked her brother.

"Someone is following us," Henry told the others. "Let's wait. The guy has to come out sometime."

They pressed up against the wall of the yogurt shop so they couldn't be seen from the inside. The figure in the baseball cap came out a few moments later. When the person spotted the Aldens, he or she dashed across the square.

Jessie recognized those blue sweatpants. "I bet I know who it is!" she declared.

"Who?" asked Benny.

"I don't know who exactly," Jessie said. "But I saw her at the sports arena this afternoon. She was sitting in the bleachers, watching us. She had on blue sweatpants."

"We can't be sure if our follower is a man or a woman," Henry stated. The runner was just a flash of blue sweatpants and brown trenchcoat. "With that coat and baseball cap, it's impossible to tell."

"Why would two people in blue sweatpants spy on us?" Jessie asked. "Why would *one* person?"

"Something is definitely weird," Violet agreed.

Benny's face was solemn under the streetlamp. "Looks like we've got another mystery to solve!"

When Grandfather joined them, the Alden children had decided not to mention

the follower. After all, as Henry had reasoned, they couldn't prove the person was actually following them.

Benny tugged at his grandfather's hand. "Katya told us she would teach us some tricks. There's a mat in that store over there like real gymnasts use."

"Let's take a look at it," said Grandfather.

The blue mat in the sports store was smaller than the mats they had seen at the gym.

"It's just right for our basement," said Violet. Like Benny, she wanted to learn to flip through the air.

"Yes, it is," James Alden agreed. "I think it's a fine idea to learn a new sport." He bought the mat, which folded into sections. Then he and Henry loaded it into the back of the station wagon.

At home, they spread it on the basement floor.

"Will you teach me how to jump up and land backward?" Benny asked Katya.

She laughed. "A backflip? That's a pretty hard trick. Let's start with some basic tumbling."

One at a time, the Alden children tried a simple forward roll.

"Keep your chin tucked in," Katya instructed Jessie. "And don't let your neck touch the mat."

When everyone had learned forward rolls, Katya showed them backward rolls.

"This is hard!" said Henry, laughing. He pushed off with his hands but flopped sideways.

Violet and Benny mastered forward and backward rolls quickly. "You both could be gymnasts," Katya praised them. "Jessie and Henry are taller, so it's harder for them, but they will learn, too."

Mrs. McGregor came down to remind the children of their bedtime.

"Katya needs her rest," she said, heading back upstairs. "Tomorrow is another long day of practice."

"Before we go, could you do a backflip?" Benny asked Katya.

"All right." She performed a perfect flip, her hands never touching the mat.

"Wow!" exclaimed Jessie. "It looks so easy."

"We will try a cartwheel," Katya told Benny. "It is more simple. I will spot you."

"What?" he asked.

"I will stand right by you, so you won't hurt yourself." She got into position beside him. "Place your hands on the mat, kick your feet up, and make them travel in a straight line like the spokes of a wheel."

Benny tried but toppled over. He kept on trying but got worse with each attempt. Soon everyone was giggling.

"We will practice every day," Katya promised him. "You will get it, Benny."

Then they went upstairs to say good night to Mrs. McGregor and Grandfather.

Katya told the Alden children good night and softly closed the guest room door.

Just beyond the stair landing was a small sitting area. A deep window seat with flowered cushions overlooked Mrs. McGregor's rose garden.

"We need to talk," Jessie said to the others.

They all piled into the window seat. Outside, bright stars were shining in the dark blue sky.

"Katya is so nice, but there's something strange about her," Jessie said.

Violet nodded. "I've noticed it, too. It's almost as if she has something to hide."

"But what?" asked Henry. "She's an athlete. She travels all over the world to gymnastic competitions."

"She's practically famous," Benny chimed in.

"But she doesn't talk about herself," said Jessie.

Henry fiddled with the cord that held the draperies. "Maybe she's modest."

"Maybe," Jessie said, unconvinced. "But I still think she's keeping a secret about something."

But what? she wondered.

What could their tiny, talented guest possibly be hiding?

The next morning, Mrs. McGregor brought in the mail.

"Here's a special airmail delivery letter for you, Katya," the housekeeper said, handing her a blue-and-red-bordered envelope.

"Oh, thank you." Katya pushed aside her oatmeal bowl to open her letter. She slit the thin envelope and pulled out a sheet of paper covered with Russian writing.

Benny stared at Katya's letter. "Those sure are funny-looking letters."

"It's Cyrillic," explained Grandfather. "That's the Russian alphabet."

Katya read silently for a few moments. Then, as she turned the page over, something fluttered to the floor.

Violet reached over to pick it up. It was a newspaper clipping in Russian. Someone had written in pencil all along the margins of the back and front of the clipping. In the center were two photos.

As the family photographer, Violet was always interested in pictures. One photo showed a huge house. The second, smaller photo showed a miniature box on a table. Even in the black-and-white photograph,

Violet thought the box was made of gold.

"You dropped this," she told Katya.

Katya's cheeks had gone bright red. "Thank you," she said, and hastily stuffed the letter and newspaper clipping into the pocket of her warm-up suit.

"Aren't you going to read the rest of your letter?" asked Benny.

"I do not want to be late for practice," Katya said, excusing herself from the table.

Jessie glanced at the clock. It was still early. Katya wasn't going to be late for practice. She obviously didn't want the Aldens to see that letter.

Who had sent the airmail letter from Russia? And why was Katya so nervous about it? None of the Aldens, not even Grandfather, could read Russian.

What did Katya have to worry about? And why had someone been following them? *So many questions*, Jessie thought. *And no answers.*

CHAPTER 4

Mystery Man Returns

The sports arena was crowded this morning, Henry noticed as they walked inside with Katya. More athletes and coaches had arrived overnight.

A press center had been set up between two sections of bleachers. Men and women with badges that said PRESS walked among the gymnasts stretching on the blue mats.

Irina, Katya's coach, came over. "You will do your beam sets first this morning. And, Katya, you must hit your mark on every routine today. The competition is three days away."

Jessie helped Katya take off her warm-up suit. "Are you worried about Friday?" she asked.

"I will do my best," Katya said matter-of-factly.

Then she began her exercises, followed by vigorous stretching. The Aldens were allowed to watch by the edge of the mat.

"You're so flexible," Henry remarked. "What is that pose you are doing?"

Katya was standing on her right leg. With ease, she picked up her left heel in her left hand and drew it up to shoulder-height, her left leg straight.

"It is called a Y scale," she replied.

Benny decided to try it. He brought his foot up, but had to bend his knee. He wobbled like a top.

Violet began to giggle. "You look like a pretzel!"

"My coach is waving me over," Katya told the Aldens. "I must go."

"We'll be waiting," Violet said. "Guess

we'd better find a seat in the bleachers. They're almost full today."

As she turned, she glanced over at the press area. Tables and chairs had been placed behind a plastic chain so only journalists and photographers would use them.

Then Violet saw something that made her stop in her tracks.

Benny nearly ran into his sister. "What is it?" he asked.

"That man over there," she said, pointing to the press section where a dark-haired man adjusted a camera. "It's Al Stockton! Our mystery man!"

Jessie and Henry stared, too.

"You're right!" Jessie declared. "It's the same man we saw in the airport."

"And the one who mistakenly took Katya's bag and came to our house to get his," Henry added. "What on earth is he doing *here*?"

As if he felt their attention, the man looked up. When he saw the Alden children, his face turned red.

Today he wasn't wearing his yellow cap,

but a wrinkled suit and a purple shirt. His press badge was clipped to an orange-and-purple tie. He was dressed differently from the way he had been at the airport, but the scowl that drew his brows together was the same.

Al Stockton unhooked the plastic chain and rushed over to the Aldens.

"What are you kids doing here?" he demanded.

Henry wondered why the man was always so rude but answered politely. "We're with our houseguest. You remember, you had her bag. She's a gymnast."

"Well, you better stay out of the press box," Al warned them. A camera was draped around his neck.

Benny looked over at the tables and chairs. "What box? I don't see any box."

"That's what the press area is called," Al told him. "It's only for media people. No nosy kids allowed."

Jessie was insulted at being called nosy. Like her older brother, she tried to be polite. "Are you a photographer?"

Al held up his camera. "What do you think? I was sent here to cover the competition for the *Register*. Now, if you kids don't mind, I've got work to do."

Then he stalked off across the floor.

Jessie put her hands on her hips. "The *nerve* of that man! *He* was the one who came running over here to talk to us! I bet he's not even a real photographer."

"Can you tell, Violet?" asked Benny.

As the family photographer, Violet knew a lot about cameras and picture-taking. She observed Al kneeling to snap shots of boy gymnasts performing on the rings that dangled from the ceiling. As much as she disliked the man, he definitely knew how to use his camera.

"He's a professional, all right," she concluded.

"Look," said Benny. "He's taking pictures of Katya."

Sure enough, the black-haired man was snapping picture after picture of Katya as she performed her complicated routine on the balance beam. He got so close that

Katya missed an aerial somersault and fell to the mat.

Although the Aldens couldn't hear from the bleachers, they could see Katya's coach, Irina, shouting at Al and drawing an invisible line on the mat. Al stepped back, scowling even more.

When another of Katya's teammates took her place on the beam, Katya came over for a quick break.

"That awful man is taking pictures of me!" she exclaimed, taking the water bottle Violet handed her.

"I know," said Jessie. "We couldn't believe it when we saw him. Of all the people to be here!"

"He's covering the competition for a newspaper," Henry said. "I hope he isn't making you nervous."

"Normally, people do not make me nervous," said Katya. "But I think he is concentrating too much on me."

Violet pulled Katya's towel from her sports bag. "It probably seems that way. Photographers have to take a lot of pictures.

Sometimes their pictures don't turn out, so they snap roll after roll."

Benny was watching the balance beam area. "He's not there now. So he must be taking pictures someplace else. Katya, that fence rail you walk on looks awfully small."

Katya laughed. "Benny, you can always make me laugh! It's a balance beam, not a fence rail. It is always four feet from the floor, sixteen feet long, and four inches wide. Our routines must have grace, poise, and courage to be scored highly."

Henry whistled. "It takes a lot of courage to do that somersault in the air like you did."

"Yes," agreed Katya. "Although I am used to it now. The difficult part about that move is that I do not know where the beam is when I am upside down. My feet could miss."

"Four inches! Something that little is easy to miss," Violet said. "Katya, your coach is waving."

"I must go." Katya gave them all a smile.

"Thank you for staying with me during practice."

This time Katya trotted over to the uneven parallel bars. She rubbed her hands with chalk, grabbed the lowest bar, and swung herself up.

Just then Al Stockton appeared and began taking pictures of Katya as she worked through her routine.

"There he is again!" Jessie cried. "Katya's right. He seems to be taking more pictures of her than anyone else."

"But why?" Violet wondered aloud. "He's supposed to take pictures of all the gymnasts, not just one."

"At least Katya is doing okay," Henry put in. "She's not looking at him."

"I wouldn't look at him, either," a strange voice said behind them.

The Aldens turned to see a young man. He had light-colored hair and wore jeans and a dark blue sweater over a white shirt. Behind wire-framed glasses, his eyes were dark blue.

"Who are you?" Benny asked.

"Lucas Tripp," said the young man. "I'm a reporter from the *Greenfield Times*. I'm covering the competition. And who might you be?"

Benny was confused by the question. "I might be anybody. But I'm really Benny Alden."

Lucas threw his head back and laughed. "Great comeback, Benny Alden!"

Jessie held out a hand. "Our brother is never at a loss for words. I'm Jessie Alden. This is Violet and Henry."

"Nice to meet you," said the reporter.

"What did you say about the man who keeps taking pictures of our friend?" Henry wanted to know.

"I was just making a joke," Lucas replied. "That dark-haired fellow doesn't get along with the rest of us in the press box."

"He took Katya's bag at the airport," Benny blurted. "Then Katya took his by mistake. And then he came to our house and wasn't very nice to Katya. He acted like she had looked in his suitcase. But she hadn't."

Lucas nodded thoughtfully. "That sounds like Mr. Al Stockton. He growls like a bear if anybody comes near his camera."

Benny giggled, then growled himself.

"Tell me about your friend," Lucas said smoothly. "I might use her as the focal point of my story."

"What do you mean?" asked Jessie. She liked Lucas but was a bit suspicious of him. Everyone seemed interested in Katya. Maybe a little *too* interested.

"It's a reporting technique," Lucas replied. "When I cover a big event, such as this competition, it helps the reader understand if I concentrate on one athlete. Tell the story from his or her point of view."

Henry looked at Jessie. He was wary of Lucas Tripp himself. "Here comes Katya now," he said. "We'll introduce you. You can ask her yourself if she wants to give an interview."

Katya was tired from her bar routine. "I

had to do it six times before I got it right,"
she said. Then she saw Lucas and smiled
shyly.

"This is Lucas Tripp," said Violet. "He's
a reporter for the *Greenfield Times*. He
wants to ask you questions."

Instantly Katya stiffened. "What questions?"

Lucas brought out his notebook and pen.
"Just about your life in Russia. . . . Is that
where you're from? Your home, things like
that."

Katya's eyes grew wary. "There is nothing to tell."

"Well, of course there is!" Lucas said
cheerfully. "Everyone has a family. What is
yours like?"

Flicking a glance at the Aldens, Katya
dropped her voice to a mumble. "You
should talk to someone more interesting
than me. I do not have a very exciting life."

"Our readers will think anything you say
is interesting," Lucas urged. "Now, tell me
about your family and where you live."

Katya's voice became a monotone, as if

she were reading from the phone book. "I live in a small town near St. Petersburg. I have a mother, a father, a brother, a sister and grandparents. I train at the gym every day. I go to school. Then I train some more."

Lucas wrote quickly. "Very good. What else?"

"That is all I have to say, Mr. Tripp. I must go now."

The Aldens and Lucas stared as Katya ran to the bleachers to pull on her warm-up suit.

"We have to go, too," Henry said. "Excuse us."

As they walked toward the bleachers, Violet said, "Katya didn't want to talk again!"

"Why is she afraid to tell people about her life?" Violet wanted to know. "It's almost like Katya isn't who she says she is."

"You've hit the nail on the head, Violet!" Jessie exclaimed. "Katya might be somebody else!"

CHAPTER 5

The Missing Music

Katya delicately pulled off a bite-sized piece of fried chicken with her fork. "This is the best thing I have ever eaten!" she exclaimed.

The Aldens were in the popular Chicken Lickin' restaurant across from Greenfield Park. Because Katya and her teammates had performed their afternoon routines so well, their coach had let them go early. Grandfather thought their guest might enjoy a meal out as a treat.

"You can pick it up," Benny said. "That's the way we eat fried chicken."

"But I'll get my fingers all greasy!" Katya said.

"Lick 'em," Benny told her. "Like the sign says!"

"Do you eat chicken in Russia?" asked Violet. Now that they wondered who Katya really was, they were more curious than ever about her background.

"Oh, yes," Katya replied. "My grandmother makes chicken Kiev. It is wonderful."

"I've had chicken Kiev," Grandfather said. "It's very tasty. A whole stick of butter is tucked inside the rolled chicken."

"And when you poke your fork into it, the butter squooshes out!" said Katya, laughing.

"Cool!" Benny said. "I like food that squooshes out."

"As long as it lands on your plate," added Jessie with a chuckle.

Katya seems much more at ease, Jessie thought. Inside the sports arena, Katya had been very tense. Maybe because she was away from other teams and reporters, Katya was loosening up. She was even telling them about her grandmother.

When the waitress refilled Grandfather's coffee mug, she announced the dessert of the day. "Chocolate cake."

Benny's eyes lit up. "Can we, Grandfather?" he asked.

"Of course," said James Alden. "I only wish I could eat as much as you do, Benny. Enjoy it while you can!"

But Katya shook her head regretfully. "I cannot eat too much before the competition."

"Then we won't have dessert, either," Benny said loyally.

Grandfather paid the check. "When the competition is over, we'll come back. Then, Katya, you may eat as much chocolate cake as you want."

She smiled at him. "Thank you, Mr. Alden. I am so lucky to have such a nice host." Then she looked away.

Violet wondered if Katya was feeling guilty about something.

"Can we go to the park now?" Benny asked.

"You bet," said Grandfather. "I have some errands to take care of in the square. I'll pick you up in an hour."

It was early evening and hardly anyone was in the park. A few people sat on the benches. Two older men played chess.

The playground was empty. Benny ran over to the slide, scrambled up the ladder, and shot down.

"Whee! Come on, Katya! This is fun!" he urged.

Katya climbed up the ladder with her gymnast's grace and slid down, giggling. "This *is* fun. I forget what it is like to play sometimes."

"Everybody needs to play," Jessie said as she and Violet chose swings.

Benny ran over to the monkey bars. He was too short to reach the first bar, so Henry gave him a boost.

"Look at me!" he cried, pulling himself along.

"Very good," said Katya.

Then she leaped onto the bars with a backward somersault. She swung from bar to bar, twisting her body in midair. When she dismounted, she arched her back, arms overhead, as if she had finished a routine for the judges.

Violet clapped. "You aren't supposed to be working!"

"That was not work," Katya said, her cheeks pink from the fresh air. "That was fun."

Then all the children clambered onto the jungle gym and sat on top, enjoying the view.

Jessie dangled her legs. It felt good to be high in the air. "There's the fountain. The water isn't turned on in the cold months, though."

Just then a bright blue disk sailed into the playground.

A big golden dog burst through the bushes near the fountain. The dog grabbed the Frisbee in his mouth, his plumy tail waving like a flag.

"Come here," cried a voice from the

trees. "You're supposed to bring the Frisbee back to me, Ralph!" A young man with light hair stepped into the clearing. He wore blue sweatpants and a gray sweatshirt.

Ralph hopped from side to side with the Frisbee still in his mouth.

The Aldens and Katya watched the scene, giggling. Clearly, Ralph wasn't going to give the Frisbee to his owner.

The young man was annoyed. "All right, show-off!"

After trotting in a perfect circle, Ralph dropped the Frisbee at his owner's feet.

"Good dog," Henry called down.

The young man looked at them for the first time, then drew back sharply in surprise. He picked up the Frisbee. "We'd better get along home, boy."

" 'Bye!" Benny said.

The young man did not look back at them or say good-bye.

Jessie stared as the pair left the park. "That man looks familiar. I know I've seen him before."

"Maybe here at the park?" Violet said.

Jessie shook her head. "I don't think so. But it wasn't long ago."

Henry swung down from the jungle gym. "Grandfather's here. You probably saw that guy in the supermarket."

Jessie hoped so. There were too many people to keep track of lately.

Denise, the American gymnast, was waiting for Katya the next morning at the Greenfield Sports Arena.

"Hi," she said. "I missed you yesterday."

"We finished practice early," Katya said. "Denise, these are my friends. Henry, Violet, Benny, and Jessie, this is Denise Patterson."

"Hi," said Denise. She had snapping dark eyes and a pert ponytail tied with a red ribbon. Like Katya, she was small for her age. "Are any of you gymnasts?"

"Katya is teaching us," Benny said. "But all I do is fall."

Denise smiled at him, showing a dimple. "Keep at it. You'll get it. We should go stretch, Katya."

The two girls worked out on the mat.

Violet scanned the room. "I wonder where Denise's mother is. She doesn't like Katya and Denise to be together."

"I don't see her," said Benny. "But there's Lucas."

Jessie couldn't believe her eyes. Lucas Tripp was wearing blue sweatpants! Exactly like the ones the red-haired woman sitting in the bleachers had worn. And just like the sweatpants worn by the mysterious figure who had followed them in the town square, and the young man they had just seen in the park.

She gripped Henry's arm. "Lucas is wearing blue sweatpants," she told him. "Is he the guy who followed us last night? You were closer to him than any of us."

"The guy — or girl — had on a coat," Henry said. "I really couldn't tell."

Lucas walked straight over to the Aldens. "You kids are just who I need to talk to."

"How can we help you?" Violet asked. Despite Lucas's cheerful manner, she was wary of the young reporter.

He pushed his glasses up on his nose and checked his spiral notebook. "I was watching Al Stockton yesterday. I don't think he works for any newspaper. He doesn't seem to be on deadline like the rest of us."

"On deadline?" quizzed Benny.

"Yes," Lucas answered. "Reporters and photographers have to have their stories and pictures finished and in by a certain time. Then the newspaper can print them. Most of us rush out of here by late afternoon. Not Al."

"Why would he tell us he's working for a newspaper if he isn't?" asked Jessie.

"Good question," said Lucas.

"Is he here today?" Violet asked.

"I haven't seen him yet," Lucas replied. "But I'll keep an eye out for him. Maybe you should, too." He glanced at his watch. "I'd better get back to work." He hurried off to where a boys' team was practicing on the parallel bars.

Henry thought of something. "Maybe Al Stockton is only pretending to work for a newspaper so he can get in the arena." He pointed to the press box.

Violet nodded. "Nobody questions why members of the press are here."

"I just wish we could get all the sweat-pants people sorted out!" Jessie said. "First that red-haired lady, then the person in the square, and then that guy in the park."

"And now Lucas," said Benny.

At that moment, a blond woman breezed past them. It was Denise's mother, Mrs. Patterson.

Denise's team and Katya's team were both practicing on the vault. The two teams were lined up. Each girl ran, hit the board, and vaulted over the horse.

Mrs. Patterson stood to one side, frowning at Katya. When it was Katya's turn, Mrs. Patterson said loudly, "That girl's hair is a mess."

The Aldens heard her and so did Katya.

It wasn't much of a remark, but it was enough to rattle Katya's concentration. Her double-twisting vault went well, but she stepped out of her landing.

Irina frowned. "Katya, I have told you, you must stick the landing." Katya bit her lip.

Jessie turned to the others. "That wasn't fair. Mrs. Patterson made Katya nervous."

Katya's next vault was perfect. So was Denise's. The two girls seemed evenly matched in that event.

Benny wished he could sail over the padded horse. Gymnastics looked like so much fun! Then he saw a movement on the other side of the horse. A man was crouched at the edge of the mat, snapping pictures.

"It's *him* again, our mystery man!" he exclaimed.

Henry saw him next. "So Al Stockton *is* here. And he seems to be taking pictures only of Katya. She was right."

"I hope he doesn't make her mess up," said Jessie.

Just then Katya gave a wail. The Aldens rushed over. Jessie thought Katya had fallen and hurt herself.

But Katya was standing over her sports

bag. Her warm-up suit spilled out of the zippered opening.

Irina reached her first. "What is it?"

"My music," Katya cried. "It is not in my bag."

"Not to worry," said Irina. "We will use my copy." The coach searched her own bag, pulling out several cassette tapes. But not the right one.

"What's going on?" Violet asked, concerned.

Now Katya was sobbing. "The music for my floor routine is gone from my bag!"

"And the backup copy I keep is missing as well," said the coach. "How very strange."

The Aldens stared at one another. Two cassette tapes kept in two different bags were missing. It wasn't just strange. It was downright suspicious.

CHAPTER 6

The Box in the Window

The Aldens rushed forward to help. They searched under the bleachers and around the equipment. They even asked other gymnasts if they had seen two cassette tapes.

But the tapes had definitely disappeared.

"It's like they walked away," said Jessie, though she knew better. Tapes don't walk off — someone had taken them.

Katya was still crying. The music was for her floor routine, her favorite event.

"We can get you another cassette," Violet offered.

"Grandfather can buy it at the music store this afternoon," added Henry.

Irina shook her head doubtfully. "Thank you. But the music for Katya's floor routine is a Russian piece. You would not be able to find it in Greenfield."

Jessie had an idea. "I bet Grandfather could find it in another city. He has friends all over."

"Perhaps," said Katya's coach. "But the competition is tomorrow. We cannot take that chance." She looked at Katya. "There is only one thing to do. We'll make up a new routine to a new piece of music."

Katya stopped crying. Her eyes widened. "How will I learn a new routine so fast?"

"Because you are the best gymnast on the team," Irina declared. "Now dry your tears. We have much work to do."

Irina flipped through the extra cassettes she had brought and selected one. "You will like this, Katya."

They began designing a new program to

the bouncy tune. Soon Katya had learned
four tumbling passes. The last pass was a
crowd-dazzler with a round-off, cartwheel,
handsprings, and three *saltos*, or aerial som-
ersaults.

Katya's shiny red leotard was damp with
sweat when Irina finally nodded with satis-
faction.

"Remember to use the entire floor," she
coached. "And give those leaps good height.
You cannot lose points on the floor routine.
It is your best event."

"We have a mat at home," said Henry.
"We'll help Katya practice some more."

Irina smiled. "Katya is lucky to have such
good friends. Go back to the Aldens' for a
break, Katya. You do not want to become
overtired."

On the way home in Grandfather's station wagon, Katya admitted her fears.

"Things happen at competitions. But I
have never had to learn a new routine one
day before the event! I spend months learning new routines. I hope I can remember it!"

"We'll write down the moves," Violet

suggested. "And you tell us where that move is when the music is playing. When you practice tonight, we'll keep saying the move."

"Good idea," said Grandfather as he pulled into the driveway. "Repetition is the key to remembering."

Benny frowned. "Repe — what?"

"Repetition," Henry answered, getting out of the car. "It's another word for 're-peat.' If you keep doing something over and over, you'll start to do it automatically. You won't have to think about it so much."

Katya nodded. "Henry is right. Irina always tells me, practice, practice, practice. Even if I think I can do it perfectly, I should practice anyway."

Inside, Mrs. McGregor had lunch ready.

"You're a little late today," the house-keeper remarked.

Grandfather explained about the missing tapes. "Katya had to learn a brand-new routine from scratch this morning."

"Well, I've made a nice hot lunch from scratch," said Mrs. McGregor. "Shepherd's pie and cranberry sauce."

Everyone washed up and sat down at the table. Then Mrs. McGregor brought in a large glass dish. Grandfather served helpings of the hamburger, vegetable, and gravy pie topped with whipped potatoes. Cranberry sauce on the side added a pleasant tang to the meal.

Since she had worked so hard that morning, Katya didn't have to return to the sports arena until late afternoon.

But when she was supposed to be napping, the children found her outside pacing around the boxcar.

"I could not lie still," she said ruefully. "So I came out here. Is it all right?"

Benny hopped up on the steps. "You can go inside our boxcar anytime you want."

Katya peeped through the doorway. "I cannot believe you really lived here."

"We did," Henry assured her. "As long as we were together, it didn't matter where we lived."

"Though Grandfather's house is a lot better," Benny said, making them all laugh.

Jessie realized that Katya had precompetition jitters. "Why don't we take a walk? You haven't seen much of our neighborhood except from the car."

"That would be nice," Katya said eagerly.

Everyone was already bundled in jackets and scarves against the chilly day. They strolled down the sidewalk, talking about everything but the competition. Benny pointed out a cat sitting on a doorstep.

"Do you have any pets?" he asked Katya.

She shook her head. "There is no room — I mean, no time to care for a pet. I am always training, you see." She fell silent.

Violet knew Katya had started to say something about not having a cat because of no room. What did she mean by that? But she couldn't question Katya further. The gymnast was nervous enough over the upcoming competition.

They had wandered out of their neighborhood and into the local shopping district. Benny pointed out the grocery store, the dry cleaner's, and the post office.

"Mrs. McGregor goes to all these places," he explained. "Sometimes we go with her."

They crossed the street and found themselves in front of a wide window. In arching gold letters, the words NEARLY NEW were painted on the glass.

"I've never noticed this store before," said Jessie, pushing back her ponytail. "Has it always been here?"

Henry nodded. "A few years. It's one of those places you never notice."

Benny pressed his nose against the window. "*I* would. Look at that cool drum set!"

He pointed to a snare drum set on a platform in the middle of the display. Surrounding the drums were other musical instruments, silver teapots, china vases, bronze statues, and many other items.

"Just what Grandfather needs," Jessie said, giggling. "You learning to play the drums!"

"Do they sell headphones here?" Violet joked.

"Looks like they sell just about everything," Henry replied, scanning the contents of the crowded display.

Jessie was staring at a small golden box

set up high on a velvet-draped shelf. She gasped.

"What is it?" Violet asked.

Jessie couldn't take her eyes off the box. "That little box. I'd like a closer look at it. Let's go in."

Violet gave her older sister a meaningful glance, then led the others inside Nearly New.

A silver-haired man sat behind a counter filled with jewelry. He glanced up from the crossword puzzle he was working on and said, "Good afternoon. May I help you?"

Benny spoke first. "How much are the drums in the window?"

The man looked at Benny over the rims of his reading glasses. "Well, young man, those particular drums aren't for sale. At least not yet."

Benny frowned. "I don't get it."

Henry did. "This is a pawnshop. People who need money bring in things like that drum set and get cash for it."

"That's right," agreed the owner. "I take the item and give them a claim ticket. The

person needs to pay back the money within a certain time period. If he doesn't, I keep the item and sell it."

"So the person who pawned the drums still has time to pay you back," Violet said, trying to understand the system.

The owner nodded.

Henry touched a saxophone. "You have so many musical instruments."

"I get a lot of them," said the owner. "And jewelry. Watches and class rings, mostly."

Jessie whispered to Violet, "Can you take Katya over there so I can talk to the man?"

"Yes," Violet whispered back. Louder, she said, "Katya, have you ever seen such pretty rings?" They moved down the display case, admiring the jewelry.

Jessie leaned closer to the owner. "That gold box in the window. What is it?"

"It's the strangest thing," said the man, scratching his chin. "I'm sure it's a fine work of art. But the young fellow who sold it to me only wanted two hundred dollars!"

"Do you remember what he looked like?" Jessie inquired.

"Let's see. He had light hair, blue eyes. And he wore blue sweatpants."

Blue sweatpants again! Did everyone in town wear them? Jessie wondered. But the description sounded familiar.

Henry and Benny gathered around her.

"Why the interest in that gold box?" Henry asked.

Sneaking a glance at Katya, who was still with Violet, Jessie replied, "It looks like the one in the newspaper picture that was in Katya's letter. Remember? She didn't want us to see it."

"I remember the picture," said Benny.

"How could a gold box in a Russian newspaper wind up in a pawnshop in Greenfield?" asked Henry.

Jessie shrugged. "I don't know. But the person who pawned it sounds like Lucas Tripp! He has light hair and blue eyes."

"A lot of people do," Henry pointed out practically. "Lucas wears glasses. The owner didn't mention glasses."

Jessie didn't want to give up the clue. "But Lucas is also interested in Katya. And she got the newspaper clipping in her letter. Maybe the printing on the clipping was a code!"

Benny was studying a small item in the display case. It was a tiny silver key with the number 11 stamped on it.

"This key," he said to the owner. "What does it go to?"

"Oh, that's my airport locker key," the man replied. "I make a lot of last-minute trips, so I keep a packed carry-on bag at the airport in a locker. This way I can leave right from the shop. And I keep my locker key in the case so I don't lose it!"

Benny felt the key he kept in his pocket. A piece of the mystery suddenly became clear.

He owned the key to an airport locker. And he found it the day Al Stockton, mystery man, ran into them at the airport. Al Stockton had dropped it.

The day they picked up Katya.

CHAPTER 7

The Switch

"Okay," said Jessie, with her hands wrapped around a mug of hot chocolate. "The big question is, did Al Stockton rent the locker and put his stuff inside and then drop the key?"

"Or did he lose the key before he could put anything inside?" Henry finished for her. "And what did he want to put in the locker? He had Katya's bag, which he thought was his. What was he using the locker for?"

The Aldens sat around the kitchen table.

Benny's key lay in the middle. They had fixed hot chocolate to drink with the plate of oatmeal raisin cookies Mrs. Mc-Gregor had made that afternoon. Katya was upstairs, resting before her special late-afternoon practice.

"Questions, questions," Jessie said. "How do we find the answers?"

"We could always go to the airport and open locker number seventeen," Violet suggested. "See what's inside."

Henry shook his head. "It's a long drive to the airport. What would we tell Grandfather we're looking for? I think we need to find out more about Al Stockton."

"I bet he took Katya's music," Benny said, reaching for his sixth cookie.

"Either him or Lucas Tripp," said Jessie. "Al is always following Katya. And Lucas keeps trying to interview her. I still think he's the one who sold the gold box to the man in Nearly New."

"The same box that was in the clipping in Katya's letter," said Violet. "This is the most complicated mystery we've ever had to solve!"

Henry got up to pour more cocoa into everyone's mugs. "I don't like talking about the case when Katya isn't around. But she's part of it somehow."

Benny sighed. He really liked Katya. If only she weren't mixed up in the mystery.

It was nearly dark when Grandfather dropped the children off at the arena. There weren't many cars in the parking lot.

Inside, only a few athletes were still working out. Most had finished their practice sessions and had gone home. The big competition was the next day.

Irina began stretching with Katya immediately. As soon as Katya had warmed up, the coach put the tape in the cassette recorder. Katya began the new floor routine.

The Alden children wandered around the arena. The press box was empty except for phones and typewriters.

"All the reporters and photographers are

back at their offices, working on the deadline," Henry guessed.

"No, there's Lucas," said Violet.

Lucas sat in the bleachers, his notebook beside him. He beckoned for the Aldens to join him.

"Are you still working?" Jessie asked him.

She looked at the young man intently, trying to match his features to the description the Nearly New shop owner gave of the man who pawned the gold box. Something was different about Lucas this evening.

"No, I'm off duty," Lucas replied. "I filed my story earlier. I just like to watch the kids perform. I want them all to win, but of course that's not possible."

"We sure hope Katya wins," Benny said. "I think she's the best."

Lucas nodded as Katya flew by on a tumbling pass. "She's very good. Let's hope the judges agree."

Jessie searched her brain for a way to bring up the gold box. "Have you ever been to Russia?"

"No, I haven't," Lucas said. "I'd love to do foreign reporting someday."

Then Jessie realized what was different about him. "You're not wearing your glasses," she commented.

He grinned. "Contacts. Sometimes I wear them instead." Slapping the wooden seat with his notebook, he rose to his feet. "I should be getting home. My dog will be wanting his supper."

"You have a dog?" Violet wanted to know. "What kind?"

"A golden Lab," Lucas answered. "All he wants to do is eat and play! See you guys tomorrow."

When Lucas had left, Jessie whirled on the others. "Lucas has a golden Lab . . . just like the guy in the park!"

Henry frowned. "But the guy in the park wasn't Lucas, Jessie. We saw him clear as day."

"I know," Jessie said, biting her lip. If only she could remember where she had seen the man in the park! "This mystery is so confusing, with gold boxes and golden

Labs and people in sweatpants. I know there's a connection somewhere!"

"We'll find it," Benny said confidently.

On the morning of the competition, Katya had only a glass of orange juice and a banana.

"I cannot eat too much before a big event," she told Mrs. McGregor.

Jessie and Violet helped Katya get ready. Today the gymnast wore her team leotard, blue with a shiny white stripe. They pulled her thick blond hair into a neat ponytail and tied it with a white ribbon. A circle of silver clips kept loose hairs from falling into Katya's face.

Then Katya pulled on a shiny satin blue-and-white warm-up suit. Her cheeks were rosy with excitement.

Then everyone piled into the station wagon, including Mrs. McGregor. Grandfather had bought tickets for the whole family.

"Too bad Watch has to stay home," said Benny.

Katya laughed. "A dog would be a funny sight on the balance beam!"

But at the main entrance of the arena, Katya stopped.

"I am supposed to meet my coach at another door, and I don't want to run into that man again," she told them. She glanced nervously at the Alden children.

Henry figured out instantly what was bothering her.

"We'll go with Katya," Henry said to Grandfather. "And then we'll find you."

Grandfather and Mrs. McGregor went inside to claim their seats.

"I don't blame you, Katya, for being afraid of running into Al Stockton," Henry said as they scurried around to the side entrance.

"Yes," said Katya. "So many things have happened. First someone pours water on my jacket. Then that man keeps taking pictures of me. Then my music was taken from my bag."

This was not a day for Katya to worry, Violet realized.

"I have a plan," she said. "Benny is about your size. How about if Benny goes inside wearing your warm-up suit?"

"Good idea, Violet," said Henry. "Katya, you can put on my coat again. It's so big, you won't get cold."

"And nobody will recognize you," Jessie added, helping Katya out of her jacket.

In minutes, Benny was wearing the blue-and-white shiny warm-up suit with the hood up over his head and Katya was bundled in Henry's large jacket. "Do I look like a girl?" he asked.

"Do not worry," Katya reassured Benny. "The boys on our Russian team wear the same suit."

Henry opened the heavy door and they filed inside. Benny went first. Katya walked behind Henry.

The arena was packed to the rafters with spectators who filled the bleachers, athletes warming up everywhere, coaches, reporters, and other people connected with the competition.

In the front, a row of men and women sat behind a table.

"Those are the judges," Katya said.

Jessie was scanning the room. "I don't see Al Stockton. Or Lucas Tripp. Looks like you're safe, Katya."

"There's Irina," said Katya, shrugging out of Henry's jacket. "Thank you for helping me. Now I must go with my teammates."

"I guess we'll go sit down with Grandfather and Mrs. McGregor," said Violet.

Benny wiggled out of Katya's suit and gave it to her so she could wear it between events. "Good luck!"

Katya blew them a kiss before running lightly across the floor toward her team.

"I can't believe Katya has done anything wrong," said Violet. "She is too nice to be mixed up in this mystery."

"I agree," said Jessie. "Maybe we'll learn the truth when the competition is over."

Henry nodded toward the girls' team bleachers. "Look who's here."

It was Mrs. Patterson, Denise's mother. She wore shiny red pants and a shirt, similar to the warm-up suits the American gymnastics team was wearing. She carried papers in her hand.

Henry got a look at the papers as she passed. "Score sheets," he said. "She's probably keeping track of Denise's scores as the judges give them."

"I bet she's keeping track of Katya's scores, too," Jessie said. "Katya and Denise are in the same class, but on opposite teams. Katya is the one Denise has to beat."

"I think we should stay down here," Benny suggested. "So we can help Katya."

"Good idea," Violet said. "If we see Grandfather, we'll tell him what's going on."

But soon the Aldens became busy watching Katya.

The first event was the uneven parallel bars. Several teams from other countries competed before the Russian team. The American team lined up behind the Russians. Mrs. Patterson stood as close to Denise as she was allowed.

Katya's teammates went first.

Then it was Katya's turn. She stood before the bars uncertainly, looking around.

"Is she scared?" Benny wanted to know.

Jessie realized what was wrong. The chalk the gymnasts rubbed on their palms before tackling the bars was missing. Someone had misplaced it . . . or taken it.

Irina was signaling to Katya, *Wait, wait.* Irina searched her bag for spare chalk, found it, and ran to Katya. Katya chalked her hands and leaped onto the bars. She began casting — swinging her body away from the lower bar. Then she swung to the higher bar, straddling it and whirling in a circle. She did a handstand just long enough for the judges to admire her form, then slid into another move.

Katya had told the Aldens each position on the bars could not be held too long. They also knew that gymnasts used chalk so their hands wouldn't blister on the wooden bars. If Katya's concentration had been hurt by the missing chalk incident, it didn't show in her magnificent dismount or in the brilliant smile she flashed the judges.

Katya received all 9.9s for her performance. Ten was the highest score.

Violet released a deep breath after the score had been posted. "Maybe this won't be so bad, after all," she said. "Her score was nearly perfect."

Jessie nudged her sister. "Think again."

Violet looked across the room. On one side of the arena, a black-haired man knelt to snap photographs. Al Stockton.

And on the other side, Lucas Tripp stood at the edge of the mat, watching Katya's every move.

Then he glanced over at the Alden children and nodded. His heels clicked on the shiny floor as he walked around the mats.

"Lucas sees us," said Benny. "He looks like he wants something."

"We'll soon find out," Henry said. "He's heading our way. And he doesn't look happy."

CHAPTER 8

The Girl in the Portrait

"Hey, there," said Lucas when he reached them. "I thought you kids would be sitting in the bleachers."

"Actually, our grandfather and our housekeeper are holding seats for us," Jessie explained. "But we thought we'd stay down here and —" She couldn't finish her sentence. Lucas was a suspect. She didn't know how he was connected to Al Stockton or Katya.

"And make sure nothing goes wrong for Katya?" Lucas concluded correctly. "It's okay. I know you kids are Katya's friends. And you think I might be one of the bad guys."

"Well, you did ask a lot of questions the other day," said Violet. "You made her nervous."

"I'm a reporter," Lucas explained. "I'm supposed to ask questions and find out facts."

Benny nodded. "So are we. We solve mysteries."

"And I'm part of the mystery, aren't I?" Lucas guessed.

"How can we trust you?" Henry said to him.

Lucas spread his hands, as if showing he had nothing to hide. "I'm not really sure what's going on around here, but your friend is involved in some way. Our buddy Al Stockton hasn't taken a single photo of anyone else today. His camera is always aimed at Katya."

Jessie looked over. Sure enough, Al was snapping pictures of Katya, who was sitting on the bench behind the vaulting horse. She and her teammates wore their warm-up suits and were sipping water.

"This is what I wanted to tell you," Lucas said. "I bumped into Al yesterday when we were leaving the arena. It was an accident, but he yelled at me. Something about touching that big bag. He's got it with him today, too."

"It's for storing extra rolls of film," Violet said, noting the camera bag slung around Al Stockton's neck.

"Maybe the guy is paranoid about it." Lucas saw the American boys' team was ready for their next event. "I'd better get back to work. Keep an eye on your friend."

"Don't worry," said Jessie. "We will."

Lucas hurried off, notebook in hand.

Henry turned to his brother and sisters. "I think we need to do a little background investigating. Right now."

"On what?" asked Violet.

"On two newspaper employees." Henry sorted through his pocket change for quarters. "Come on."

They walked the length of the arena to

the concession area. Floor music blared from loudspeakers as one group of gymnasts performed floor routines, while another group did balance beam sets, and yet another worked out on the rings.

"I don't know how the gymnasts can concentrate," Violet remarked, "with all this action going on around them."

"They must be used to it," said Jessie as they walked past a counter that sold hot dogs and nachos.

"I smell food," said Benny, sniffing the air.

Violet giggled. "You just had breakfast!"

"I can eat a hot dog anytime," he said.

Henry headed for the bank of telephones. Local phone books bound in metal covers were mounted beneath the row of phones. Jessie looked up the first number for him.

Henry punched it in. "Hello," he said when someone on the other end answered. "Is Lucas Tripp there today?"

He paused, then said, "No, that's okay. Thanks very much." He hung up.

"Well?" prompted Violet.

"Lucas works at the *Greenfield Times* as a reporter, just like he told us," Henry replied. "And he's out on assignment, the secretary said."

Jessie read off the second number and Henry punched it in. This time he asked, "Is Al Stockton there today?"

The pause was much shorter. Henry said thanks and carefully hung up the receiver.

"The receptionist at the *Register* has never heard of Al Stockton," he said with excitement. "He's never worked there a day in his life! Al Stockton is a phony!"

"We can scratch Lucas off our suspect list for now," said Jessie. "But how do Al and Katya fit into this case?"

Benny pulled out the silver locker key. "Maybe this is the answer. I mean, I found it the day we got Katya at the airport. And Al Stockton was there, too."

"Benny's right!" said Violet. "We're overlooking the most important clue of all! Katya flew to America from Russia. Al Stockton was on her flight from New York."

"I'll bet our mystery man also flew to

New York from Russia," Henry said, following his sister's thinking. "As soon as Al got off the plane," Henry continued, "he rented a locker. I think he brought something back from Russia to put in that locker."

Benny waved the key. "And then he lost this."

"Maybe he thinks Katya has the gold box," Jessie said. "That's why he keeps following her around! He wants it back. So he's pretending to work for a newspaper."

"So," said a voice behind them. "You've found out the truth."

Jessie jumped. But it wasn't Al Stockton standing behind them.

It was Lucas Tripp.

"I — uh," she stammered. Did they take Lucas off their suspect list too soon?

"I overheard Henry's calls and part of your conversation just now," the young man said, a little embarrassed. "Our pal Al isn't employed at the *Register* after all. Good work! I should have looked into that myself days ago. It seems that while I've been so busy on this gymnastics story, a real mystery has been unfolding."

Jessie breathed a sigh of relief. Lucas was okay. "The competition people would probably have kept Al out if they saw this unidentified guy taking pictures of Katya."

"It's not that hard to get a press pass," Lucas said. "Especially if he's worked for a paper somewhere else. Nobody questions a photographer with good credentials."

"So what do we do now?" Violet wanted to know.

"Unfortunately, I've got to get back to that event I'm covering," Lucas said, running his hand through his light hair. "I think you kids should make sure Al doesn't do anything to upset Katya. And I'd like to hear more about that gold box you mentioned. I'll see you later."

He reluctantly hurried off once more.

"I think Lucas is okay," said Jessie. "It looks like we'd better get moving. The teams in Katya's class are heading for the balance beam."

Sure enough, all the junior girls from

various countries were settling in lines near the balance beam. Mrs. Patterson, score sheet under her arm, redid her daughter Denise's hair, adding a fresh red ribbon.

Denise smiled at Katya and gave her the thumbs-up sign. Katya returned the signal.

"They're wishing each other good luck," Henry observed. "It's nice they're friends even though they are on opposite teams. I can't believe Katya is mixed up in anything mysterious. She's just so nice."

"I know," Jessie agreed.

Just then Mrs. Patterson said something to her daughter. Reluctantly, Denise faced forward, so she couldn't see Katya.

"That woman acts like she's running this competition," Violet remarked. "How could it hurt Denise's chances to smile at Katya?"

"That's the way some mothers are, Katya told us," Henry reminded them. "They take sports more seriously than their kids."

"I think they are starting," Violet said, noticing the coach lining up the first team to compete. "Let's go over."

As the Aldens left the concession area,

they found themselves mingling with reporters, photographers, and other people
moving toward the balance beam area. The
difficult beam event always drew a large
crowd.

Someone bumped into Benny, hard. He
went down on one knee.

Henry was at his brother's side instantly.
"Are you all right, Benny?"

"I'm fine," Benny said, staring at the
floor. Big shoes that needed polishing were
right in front of him.

A voice growled, "Look what you did!"

This time the voice belonged to Al
Stockton. Now he was down on his knees,
too, scooping scattered rolls of film and
special lenses back into his camera bag.

"You made me drop my bag!" he com-
plained. "If any of these lenses are
cracked — "

"I'm sorry," Benny said. "But you ran
into me." He tried to help by picking up
loose photos that had slid from a side
pocket.

"Leave those alone!" Al lunged for a sheaf of pictures in Benny's hand.

"Take it easy," Henry said, coming to his brother's defense. "He's only trying to help."

"You kids are always getting in my way!" Al accused. "Now give me those pictures."

Benny gave the man his pictures. But two slipped from the hastily gathered stack. They landed faceup on the floor.

Benny stared.

One picture showed a huge, beautiful mansion with a circular driveway in front.

The second picture was an indoor shot of a fancy living room. A vase of flowers stood on a table. Above the table was a portrait of a young girl. The girl wore a fancy-looking red dress. Her blond hair curled on her shoulders.

The girl looked exactly like Katya Ludskaya!

Al quickly snatched the pictures and stuffed them in his camera bag. "Next time," he warned, "stay out of my way!"

Then he hurried off to the balance beam area.

Violet helped Benny up. "Honestly, that man is so rude. Are you okay?"

"Did you see the pictures?" Benny asked, his fall forgotten.

"I sure did," Jessie answered excitedly. "The one of the house — I know where I've seen it before!"

"Where?" asked Henry. In the flurry of dealing with Al Stockton, he hadn't gotten a good look at the two photographs.

"It's the same house in the newspaper clipping that was in Katya's letter from Russia!" Jessie declared.

"Why would Al Stockton have a picture of a Russian house in his bag? The same house that was in a newspaper clipping in Katya's letter?" Henry inquired.

"Did you see the *second* picture?" Benny insisted.

Jessie nodded. "In it was a painting of a girl."

"And the girl looked a lot like Katya!" Benny said.

Henry whistled. "Now things are really getting complicated. I bet the room in the second picture is in the mansion. And if the girl in the portrait is Katya, she obviously lives in the mansion."

"So Katya is really a rich girl pretending to be a gymnast?" Violet asked.

Jessie shook her head. "I don't think she's pretending to be a gymnast. She's too good. But if she's rich, she wouldn't need to live with an American family for this competition. Why is she staying with us?"

Benny thought he knew the answer. "To hide who she really is."

Now they all looked over at the balance beam. Katya's team wasn't performing yet, but they would soon.

"We'll have to wait until after the competition to find out Katya's identity," Henry said.

Violet stared at the black-haired man, who was watching Katya intently. "And so will Al Stockton."

CHAPTER 9

The Competition

K atya was poised on the mat at one end of the balance beam. She looked toward the judges. The head judge signaled that they were ready. Then Katya took a deep breath and raised her arm in return.

With a swift move she straddled the end of the beam. Her hands on either side of the narrow wood, she eased into a hand-stand, then came down into a V-sit.

Violet Alden held her breath. She knew that Katya's routine was one minute and twenty-five seconds. If it was too long or too short, the judges would take points from her score.

"Now she's changing directions," Jessie said, watching Katya pivot smoothly on one foot.

That was another requirement. Katya's eyes were straight ahead as she waved her arms gracefully and pointed her toes. Next she performed a stride leap, springing up and down into a split. A headstand turned her in the opposite direction. Then, in a flurry of cartwheels, Katya was across the beam. She dismounted with a round-off.

Standing on the mat a second to gain her balance, she raised her arms and arched her back. She had stuck the landing!

"She did it!" Benny cried, applauding along with the audience.

The Aldens eagerly awaited the five judges' scores. Katya received 9.7 from four judges and a 9.8 from one.

"Very good scores," Henry commented. "If Al Stockton is bothering Katya by being here, it's not affecting her routines."

The rest of Katya's team performed, and

then it was the American team's turn. Denise was in the lead position, getting the same marks as Katya.

Jessie watched Mrs. Patterson write down the scores on her score sheet. She did not look happy. Jessie figured the woman wanted her daughter to score higher than Katya. As far as Jessie could tell, Katya and Denise were evenly matched.

The announcer called for an intermission. The Alden children used the opportunity to find Grandfather and Mrs. McGregor.

"There you are!" said the housekeeper. "We wondered where you've been."

"We didn't mean for you to worry," Violet apologized. "But we need to keep an eye on Katya. She — " Without revealing the question of Katya's mysterious identity, Violet continued, "She's nervous and likes to have us nearby."

Grandfather nodded. "I understand. You have become friends this week. She's a very nice girl."

I only hope she's telling the truth about who

she is, Violet thought. She would hate to have her grandfather disappointed.

"Katya's scores are excellent," Grandfather said. "She did well on the vault and aced her bar and beam routines."

"I hope she wins," Mrs. McGregor said firmly.

"They're starting again," Benny said. "We'd better get over there."

The last event was the floor routine. The audience buzzed with excitement. Floor routines gave the gymnasts a chance to show their best skills.

Music blared from the loudspeakers. The audience clapped with the beat as the first gymnast performed.

Soon it was Katya's turn again. She stood at the corner of the huge blue mat, waiting for her music. Jessie could see her coach frantically rummaging through a bag.

Katya threw a worried glance at Irina.

"I bet the tape with Katya's new music is gone again!" Violet declared.

Jessie pulled a cassette from her pocket. "Well, this time we're prepared." She strode over to Irina. "We made an extra copy, just in case."

A look of immense relief broke over the coach's face. "Thank you very much. You are such a good friend to Katya." Then she hurried to the music station.

In seconds, Katya's music poured from the loudspeakers. Katya smiled and began her first tumbling pass.

"Good thing you thought of making an extra copy of Katya's tape," Henry praised Jessie.

"Too many weird things have happened at this competition," Jessie said modestly. "I just wanted to make sure nothing else went wrong."

"It's awfully funny how Katya's music keeps disappearing," said Benny.

Jessie didn't think it was funny at all. She couldn't keep her eyes on all the suspects at the arena, but she had a good idea who the culprit was.

On her last tumbling pass, Katya was even better than she'd been in practice. The Alden children had worked with her the night before in their basement, until Katya had perfected every move.

Now Katya stopped precisely at the far corner, not stepping out of bounds, and raised her arms in the air.

The audience loved her routine. They stamped and cheered. Katya bowed to both sides of the arena. She looked happy, as if she knew she had performed well.

The judges must have felt the same way, Henry thought as he watched the white cards flip over. Every judge scored her floor routine at 9.9, the highest score received that day on the junior team.

Katya sat down with her teammates, who patted her on the back. The American team performed next. Denise's floor routine was good, but not as daring as Katya's. Denise received scores of 9.7 and a 9.8. Jessie saw Mrs. Patterson's face fall when the scores were displayed.

"The competition is over for Katya's class," Henry told the others. "It's time for the awards."

At the judges' table, the men and women

conferred briefly. Then the announcer spoke.

"Ladies and gentlemen," he said. "First place for the all-around gymnast goes to Katya Ludskaya of Russia!"

The Aldens clapped harder than anyone. Benny even whistled as Katya climbed up on the stage to receive her medal.

Denise Patterson was the second-place winner and a girl from the Romanian team won third. Katya and Denise hugged each other as photographers snapped the winners' picture.

"This is so exciting!" Violet cried, still clapping.

Next, the award was announced for the best team performance.

The American gymnasts took the first-place medal, with Katya's team winning second. Once more, Katya and Denise hugged each other.

"There're even!" Benny cheered.

"And they're friends," Jessie said. "Even though Denise's mother tried to keep them apart."

When the ceremony was over, Katya and Denise came over to the Aldens. The girls glowed with happiness, wearing their medals.

"Congratulations," Henry said. "You both were great."

"Thanks," said Denise. "Katya and I are going to write to each other. We'll probably see each other at other competitions, too."

"Uh-oh," said Katya. "Your mother is coming."

"I'd better get back to my team," Denise said. "See you later, Katya."

Mrs. Patterson swept in their direction. But instead of following her daughter, Mrs. Patterson halted in front of Katya.

"I want to apologize," she said. "I've done some terrible things the last few days."

"You were the one who poured water on Katya's warm-up jacket," Jessie said. "And you hid the chalk for the uneven parallel bars."

Mrs. Patterson nodded, ducking her head

in shame. "I also took your music for your floor routine. I didn't mean to hurt you . . . I just wanted Denise to win."

"She did win," Katya said. "She is a very good gymnast."

"But not as good as you," said the woman. "I watched you during the early practice sessions. You have a drive that Denise doesn't."

Jessie turned to her. "Were you wearing blue sweatpants and a red wig the other day?"

Mrs. Patterson blushed. "Yes. Sometimes I put on a disguise to check out Denise's competition. Well . . ." She was too embarrassed to say anything else. "I'd better find my daughter."

"Unbelievable!" Violet exploded when the woman had left. "She did all that to help her daughter win!"

"It didn't matter," Henry pointed out. "Katya won anyway."

"I'm glad we solved the gymnastics part of the mystery," Benny said. "But we still have lots of questions left."

"Like why Al Stockton is following you everywhere," Violet said to Katya.

"He has looked at me strangely ever since the day he came to your house to pick up his bag," Katya remarked nervously. "I do not know why he keeps watching me."

"Maybe we can find out," Henry said thoughtfully. "I have an idea."

"What is it?" asked Jessie.

"Remember those pictures Benny saw that fell out of Al Stockton's camera bag?"

Jessie nodded, then explained to Katya about the photographs. She didn't mention that the photograph of the house was the same house in Katya's letter.

"We're going to make one of the pictures come to life," said Henry.

"How are we going to do that?" Benny wanted to know.

"If Mrs. Patterson can disguise herself, so can Katya!"

The children went back to the concession area. Henry and Benny waited outside the ladies' rest room while Jessie, Violet, and Katya went inside.

When the girls emerged, Violet was wearing Katya's warm-up suit.

Katya had on Violet's purple jumper and pink long-sleeved turtleneck. Her ponytail had been combed out. Her gleaming blond hair fell softly to her shoulders.

"Here comes Al Stockton," Henry said. "Right on cue."

Jessie gave Katya a little push forward. "It'll be all right. We're right behind you."

Katya walked into the bright lights of the concession area.

Al turned and stared at her, his jaw dropping.

"You!" he said hoarsely. "I knew it was you when I saw you in the airport! You've followed me all the way to America!"

CHAPTER 10

Benny's Trick

K atya's blue eyes were like saucers. "*I* followed *you*!" she declared unbelievingly. "*You* have been following *me*!"

Jessie let out the breath she had been holding.

"You looked scared when you first saw Katya," she said to him. "Why?"

"She reminded me of somebody," Al replied. "In that dress and all."

Henry said, "A girl in a painting, maybe?"

Al's eyes narrowed. "You snoopy kids act like you know something."

"We are not snoops," Benny corrected. "We solve mysteries."

"We'll start with the day you got off the plane," Henry said. "We were waiting for Katya, who was on the same flight."

Violet took over the story. "You grabbed her bag."

"That was a mistake!" Al insisted.

"Yes, it was," Violet agreed. "Especially since there was something in your bag you had stolen."

Now Al stiffened. "What are you talking about?"

At that moment, Lucas Tripp came up. This time he was wearing his glasses. "Mr. Stockton," he said. "I see you're still here."

"Of course I'm here," Al said defensively. "I'm covering this competition for my newspaper."

"Is that so?" Lucas countered. "The Alden kids found out you don't work at the *Register*. In fact, the receptionist at the paper had never even heard of you."

Al's face changed. His expression became less angry and more worried as he realized he was in trouble. "What else do you kids know?"

"We know you lost this." Benny dangled the silver locker key. "I found it on the floor in the airport."

"A key doesn't prove anything," Al said. "That locker could be empty."

"Aha! You know it's a locker key," Henry said. "You dropped the key before you could put anything in it. And then you found you had the wrong duffel."

Al shook his fist at Katya. "You found the gold box, didn't you? You stole it from my bag!"

"What gold box?" asked Katya. She looked confused.

Jessie turned to the black-haired man. "Katya doesn't know anything about the gold box. She just happened to pick up your bag by mistake. Just like you picked up hers by mistake. When she saw men's clothes were in it, she closed it. She didn't go snooping. She never even saw the gold box."

"All right," said Al with resignation. "I

went to Russia on a phony magazine assignment. It's my scam. The way I operate. The owners of fancy mansions let me photograph their homes. While I was in Russia, I worked this mansion and swiped that little gold box off a table."

"You smuggled it into this country," Henry guessed. "In your suitcase."

"Yes," Al admitted. "I have a partner who helps me find wealthy buyers who don't ask embarrassing questions."

Benny spoke up. "But you lost the box."

Al frowned. "When I realized I had this girl's bag, I hurried to your house the next morning, hoping she had mine."

"But something frightened you," Violet interrupted.

"Her!" Al pointed at Katya. "There was a painting in the mansion in Russia of a little girl. *She* looks just like the girl in the painting! It was like she was haunting me!"

"I think it was your guilty conscience, Mr. Stockton, that was haunting you," Lucas said, crossing his arms over his chest.

"Tell us about the box. What happened to it? Why did you rent a locker?"

"To put the box in," said Al. "I live with my aunt and uncle in Rockwell. My aunt goes through my room sometimes. I didn't want her to find the box, so I planned to hide it in the locker until I could meet my partner. We'd pick it up together. But first I called him to tell him I was home."

"That's when you saw Katya," stated Benny. "In the airport."

"She startled me," Al confessed. "And some guy wanted the phone. So I decided to go home and bring the box back later, when I wasn't so rattled. But then I found out I had the wrong bag! So when I got my bag back the next day, I stopped at a pay phone to call my partner again. I wanted to let him know I had the bag back. When I returned to my car, I checked my bag for the box and it was gone! You took it!" he accused Katya.

"None of us believe that Katya stole the box," said Henry. "It must have been someone else. The same someone who took it to the Nearly New pawnshop."

"I've been doing a little investigating myself," said Lucas. "I called the owner of the pawnshop where you said you saw the gold box — " Lucas looked sheepishly at the Aldens. "I can't resist a mystery, either."

"The box was pawned?" Al said incredulously.

Lucas continued, "The young man who stole it from Al's car needed rent money. He told the pawnshop owner he was between jobs. His landlady was threatening to kick out him and his dog."

"The dog!" Jessie exclaimed. "He was the guy we saw in the park playing Frisbee with Ralph, the dog. I knew I'd seen him somewhere before! He was the man waiting to use the phone in the airport!"

"That's right." Lucas nodded. "The man's name is Chuck. After you kids were in Nearly New, the owner became suspicious and took the gold box out of the window. He was afraid it was stolen property."

"It was stolen twice," Violet said. "First

by Al, then by Chuck. But how does this Chuck fit into the mystery?"

"That's what I've been busy finding out," said Lucas. "Chuck overheard Al talking about the box on the phone in the airport. It was just a coincidence that Chuck was hanging out there, hoping to find some loose change. Then he followed Al to his house in Rockwell. But Al took his bag in the house that night. The next morning Chuck followed Al again when he went to the Aldens'. When Al stopped at the pay phone, Chuck took the box from Al's duffel in his car and pawned it."

"What happened to Chuck?" Jessie asked.

"The pawnshop owner had his address," said Lucas. "The police have picked him up for questioning. The gold box is very valuable. The Russian owner is frantic to get it back."

"And the wealthy Russian owner is not related to Katya?" Jessie asked.

Everyone turned to look at Katya.

"I am not related to *anyone* wealthy," said Katya and she looked at the floor.

Benny put his hand on her shoulder.

Al groaned. "I've been double-crossed by a bunch of kids and a broke guy with a Frisbee-playing dog!"

"You followed us," Henry realized. "That was you in the town square the other night. You were wearing sweatpants and a trench-coat."

"And you followed Katya during practice," Violet put in. "You kept taking her picture."

"I couldn't believe she was the same girl who lived in the fancy house in Russia," Al said. "You saw the picture of the painting in that house. Katya looks just like that girl. I kept comparing the photos I took of Katya to that picture, but I still wasn't sure."

"What were you going to do?" Lucas demanded.

"Take the gold box back from her," Al said matter-of-factly. "If Katya was the daughter of the Russian guy, I figured she followed me to America. She was also on the gymnastics team. But when the competition was over, she'd blow the whistle on me. I had to get the box back and disappear."

"You've done this before, haven't you?" Benny guessed.

The corners of Al's mouth turned down. "At least it *was* a good scam."

"Well, it's over now," Lucas said, stepping closer. "I've called the police. They're on their way."

Suddenly Al bolted. He shot between Henry and Lucas.

Benny knew Al would blend into the crowd in seconds. He couldn't run as fast as the older man. But maybe he could do something to slow him down.

Remembering what Katya had taught him, he planted his hands on the floor and did a lopsided cartwheel.

Al tripped over Benny. His escape route was blocked long enough for Lucas and Henry to clutch the man's arms.

"Well done!" Katya cried, hugging Benny.

"I still fell," Benny said. He wished he could learn that trick.

At that moment, Grandfather, Mrs. Mc-Gregor, and the police arrived on the scene.

Grandfather looked at his grandchildren. "I don't even have to ask," he said, smiling. "You've just solved another mystery!"

"We'll tell you all about it, Grandfather," said Benny. "If you'll take us to Joe's Pizza." Now that he had helped save the day, Benny realized he was starving.

Everyone laughed.

"Joe's Pizza it is," said Grandfather.

"We didn't like keeping the mystery from you," said Jessie to Grandfather and Mrs. McGregor. "But we needed to find out more about Katya. We thought she might be trying to hide something. Sorry, Katya," she added to the gymnast.

Katya pushed her plate away. She had eaten more pizza than Benny, to his astonishment.

"It is all right," she said. "I have not been a very good houseguest."

"Of course you have," Mrs. McGregor protested.

Katya ducked her head. "I have not told you the truth about myself."

Jessie held her breath. Had they been wrong about Katya after all?

"If you feel comfortable, why don't you tell us about it now," Grandfather said gently.

"I did not like talking about my life back home," Katya said. "When you and Mr. Lucas asked me those questions, I felt nervous."

"Why?" asked Violet. "We were just curious about how you live in Russia."

"I was afraid you would not understand," Katya confided. "You see, I live in a small apartment with my large family. It is very cramped. I share a bed with my sister. My mother works to help pay for my training. My grandmother baby-sits the little ones so we can take the train every day to my gym."

"What's wrong with that?" Henry asked.

"When I arrived in America, I thought everyone was rich," said Katya. "When I saw your boxcar, I knew everyone is not rich — but I was still embarrassed." Her cheeks turned pink. "I even tried to hide a letter my grandmother sent because part of it was written on a page of our local newspaper. We cannot afford good writing paper."

Jessie patted Katya's arm. "The newspaper your grandmother sent showed pictures of the house Al visited and the gold box he stole. That was a good clue!"

"I am glad I could help," Katya said. She smiled warmly at the Aldens. "I won more than a medal today. This trip taught me that I am lucky, maybe luckier than the little rich girl you all think I resemble in that photograph. I am lucky because I have the love of my family. Just like you do."

"Nothing is more important than family," said Grandfather.

"That's right!" declared Benny. "Family and food."

Outside, they strolled around the square.

"You know what I *still* don't understand," Jessie muttered to herself. "Why is it everyone was wearing blue sweatpants?"

At the teddy bear shop, Grandfather and Mrs. McGregor went inside.

While the Alden children and Katya waited outside, Henry looked into the window of a sporting goods and clothing store and started to laugh.

"Look, Jessie," he said.

There in the window stood a mannequin dressed in a blue sweatshirt and sweatpants. SALE ITEM OF THE WEEK, a sign proclaimed, and in smaller letters, AVAILABLE IN BLUE ONLY. As the children broke out laughing, Grandfather and Mrs. McGregor came out of the teddy bear store with the bear Katya had admired.

"A going-away present," Grandfather said. "To remember us by."

"I will never forget any of you," Katya exclaimed. "I am going to name him — Benny!"

"Yippee!" Happily, Benny performed a perfect cartwheel.

Everyone clapped.

Jessie was glad this mystery had been solved. But another could be arriving by train or plane . . . or they could find one in their own neighborhood.

GERTRUDE CHANDLER WARNER discovered when she was teaching that many readers who like an exciting story could find no books that were both easy and fun to read. She decided to try to meet this need, and her first book, *The Boxcar Children*, quickly proved she had succeeded.

Miss Warner drew on her own experiences to write the mystery. As a child she spent hours watching trains go by on the tracks opposite her family home. She often dreamed about what it would be like to set up housekeeping in a caboose or freight car — the situation the Alden children find themselves in.

When Miss Warner received requests for more adventures involving Henry, Jessie, Violet, and Benny Alden, she began additional stories. In each, she chose a special setting and introduced unusual or eccentric characters who liked the unpredictable.

While the mystery element is central to each of Miss Warner's books, she never thought of them as strictly juvenile mysteries. She liked to stress the Aldens' independence and resourcefulness and their solid New England devotion to using up and making do. The Aldens go about most of their adventures with as little adult supervision as possible — something else that delights young readers.

Miss Warner lived in Putnam, Connecticut, until her death in 1979. During her lifetime, she received hundreds of letters from girls and boys telling her how much they liked her books.